Text copyright © 1990 by Harriet Ziefert
Illustrations copyright © 1990 by Mavis Smith
Printed in Singapore for Harriet Ziefert, Inc.
All rights reserved.
1 2 3 4 5 6 7 8 9 10
First Edition
CIP data available.
ISBN 0-06-026894-8.—ISBN 0-06-026895-6 (lib. bdg.)
Library of Congress Catalog Card Number: 90-4456

I WANT TO SLEEP IN YOUR BED!

Harriet Ziefert · Pictures by Mavis Smith

Harper & Row, Publishers

It was dark. It was night.
It was time for everyone to go to sleep.

Mommy covered the bird cage.
"Good night, sleepy parakeet," she said.

Then Mommy carried the baby upstairs and put him in his crib. She wound the music box. "Good night, sleepy baby," she whispered.

Susan kissed the dog good night.
Daddy told him to go to his bed.
"Good night, sleepy dog."

Daddy carried Susan to her bed.
He pulled up the covers and kissed her
on the forehead. "Good night, sleepy Susan."

Then Mommy and Daddy went into
their room and closed their door.
"Good night, Mommy and Daddy."

Soon everyone was fast asleep—

everyone but Susan.

Susan stood outside her parents' door
and cried, "I want to sleep in your bed!"

Daddy opened the door and said,
"Everyone sleeps in their own bed."

Susan cried and cried.
"But I want to sleep in your bed!"

Daddy carried Susan to her room.

"Children sleep in their own beds," said Daddy.
"And mommies and daddies sleep in their own bed."

Daddy pulled up Susan's covers and tucked her in.
He sat with her for awhile. "Close your eyes,"
he whispered. "Soon you'll be asleep."

Then he left the room.

Susan closed her eyes. But she couldn't fall asleep.
She threw off her covers and ran to her parents' door.

Susan cried, "I want to sleep in your bed.
I can't go to sleep in mine."

"Yes, you can," said Susan's mother. "Let's take
a walk and see how everyone is sleeping."

"The sleepy parakeet is asleep in the parakeet cage."

"The sleepy dog is asleep in the dog bed."

"And your sleepy brother is asleep in his crib."

Then Mommy walked Susan to her room.
She pulled up the covers and tucked her in.

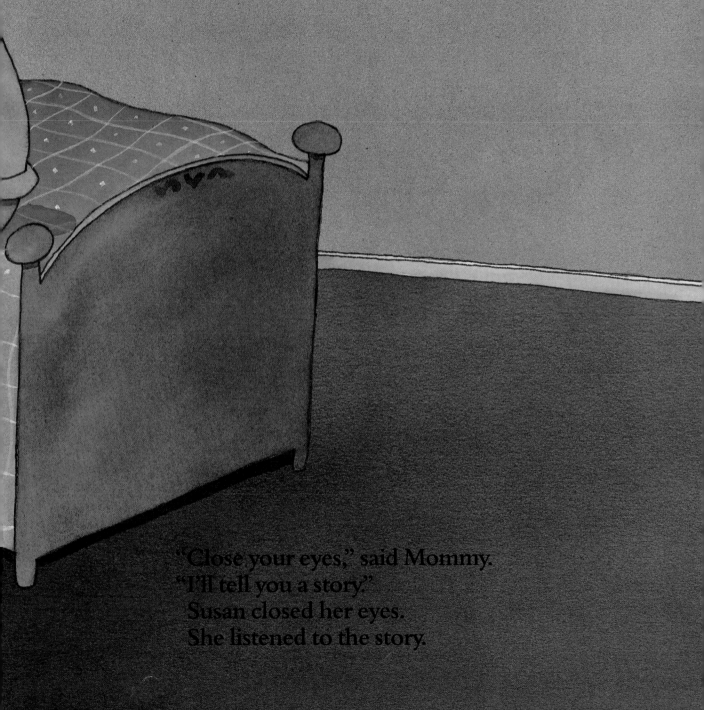

"Here's your doll," said Mommy.
"I don't want my doll," said Susan.
"Aren't you sleepy?" said Mommy.
"I am sleepy," said Susan.
"But I don't know how to fall asleep."

"Close your eyes," said Mommy.
"I'll tell you a story."
Susan closed her eyes.
She listened to the story.

Susan heard her mother leave the room.
She opened her eyes.

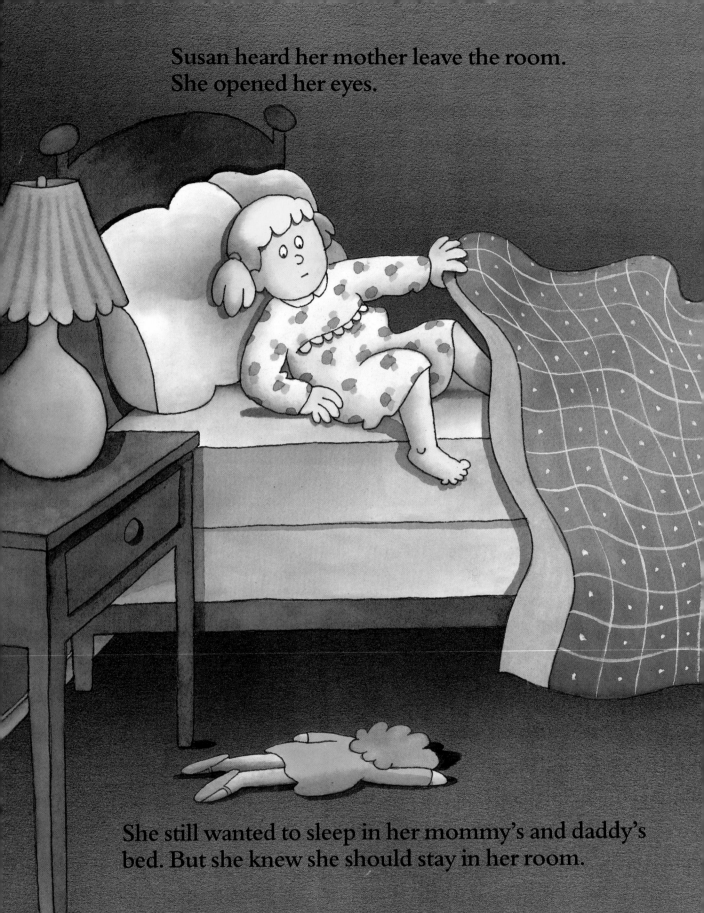

She still wanted to sleep in her mommy's and daddy's
bed. But she knew she should stay in her room.

So she got out of bed and picked up her doll.
"Now I'm going to put you to sleep," she said.

Susan dragged her doll's small bed over so that
it was next to her own big bed.

Susan pulled up the covers and tucked her doll in.
"Close your eyes," she whispered. "I'll tell you a story."

And Susan began a story about a little girl who didn't want to sleep in her own bed.

But Susan was so tired that soon she fell asleep.
Good night, sleepy Susan.